P9-BYG-897

COLUMBIA PICTURES PRESENTS A RED WAGON AND FRANKLIN/WATERMAN PRODUCTION A FILM BY ROB MINKOFF STARRING: GEENA DAVIS "STUART LITTLE 2" HUGH LAURIE AND JONATHAN LIPNICKI MUSIC BY ALAN SILVESTRI EXECUTIVE PRODUCERS JEFF FRANKLIN AND STEVE WATERMAN ROB MINKOFF GAIL LYON JASON CLARK BASED UPON CHARACTERS FROM THE BOOK "STUART LITTLE" BY E.B. WHITE STORY BY DOUGLAS WICK AND BRUCE JOEL RUBIN SCREENPLAY BY BRUCE JOEL RUBIN PRODUCED BY LUCY FISHER AND DOUGLAS WICK DIRECTED BY ROB MINKOFF COLUMBIA PICTURES

StuartLittle.com

Stuart Little 2™: The Movie Storybook
TM & © 2002 Columbia Pictures Industries, Inc. All rights reserved.
Adapted by Julie Michaels
HarperCollins®, ✸®, and HarperFestival® are registered trademarks of HarperCollins Publishers Inc.
Printed in the U.S.A.
Library of Congress catalog card number: 2001093964

Cover design by Max Maslansky
Interior design by Gavin Morris

10 9 8 7 6 5 4 3 2 1
❖
First Edition

www.Stuart.Little.com
www.harperchildren.com

STUART LITTLE 2™

The Movie Storybook

Adapted by Julie Michaels
Unit photography by Peter Iovino
CG imagery by Sony Pictures Imageworks

HarperFestival®
A Division of HarperCollinsPublishers

Chapter 1

Stuart's New Friend

Stuart Little was part of a loving family.
The Littles lived all together in the big city.

Stuart lived with his mother; father; brother, George; and baby sister, Martha. Stuart was the littlest Little.

Even though Stuart was little, he
liked to play the games that other boys
his age played, including soccer.

"It's going to be great!" cheered
Stuart before his first game.

A big breakfast would help Stuart be ready to play. Of course, most breakfasts were big to Stuart!

At the soccer game, Stuart was happy when his coach finally put him on the field to play. Stuart was ready to help his team.

But when Stuart ran onto the field,
the ball hit him so hard that he stuck to
it and went flying into the goal.

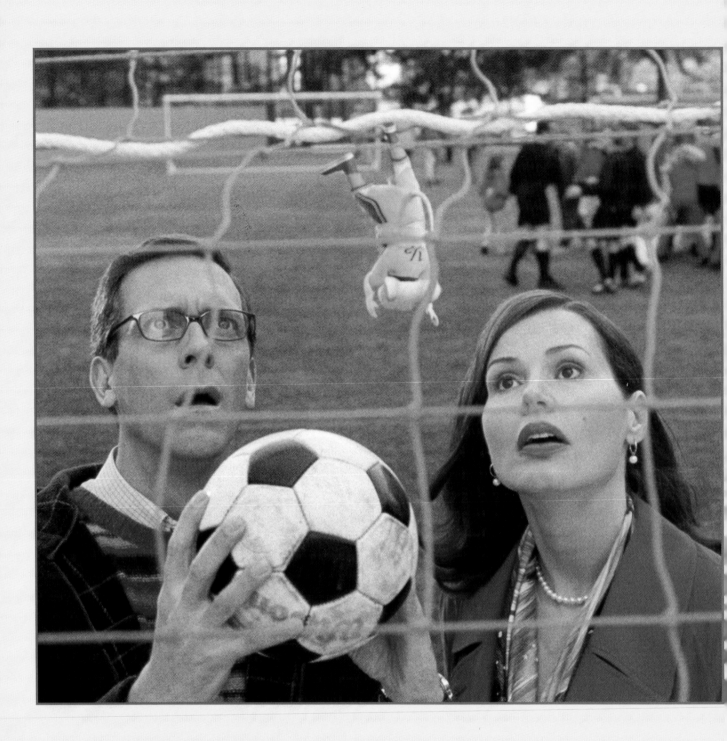

"Do I get an assist?" groaned Stuart.

Mrs. Little worried that Stuart would get hurt. "He looks so small out there— so lacking in 'bigness.' Does he really have to play soccer?" she asked.

"We have to give him room to grow," said Mr. Little.

Mrs. Little thought Stuart had found a nice, safe hobby in building toy models. Stuart and his brother had already built a boat and a car. Now they were building a plane.

But something went wrong. . . .
"I'm in the air!" cried Stuart, as the
plane suddenly took off.

Stuart flew through his house and straight out the door. His worried family hurried after him.

The plane took Stuart into a nearby park.
"Mayday! Mayday!" cried Stuart. "Nuns
at twelve o'clock."

Stuart tried to keep calm. *There must be some way to land*, he thought to himself.

Stuart found a way—he flew straight into a thick bush. *Swoosh-smash-crash!* Luckily, Stuart was not hurt.

Mr. Little tried to make Stuart feel
better. "The thing about being a Little
is you can always see the bright side,"
he said. "Every cloud has a silver lining."
Every cloud? wondered Stuart.

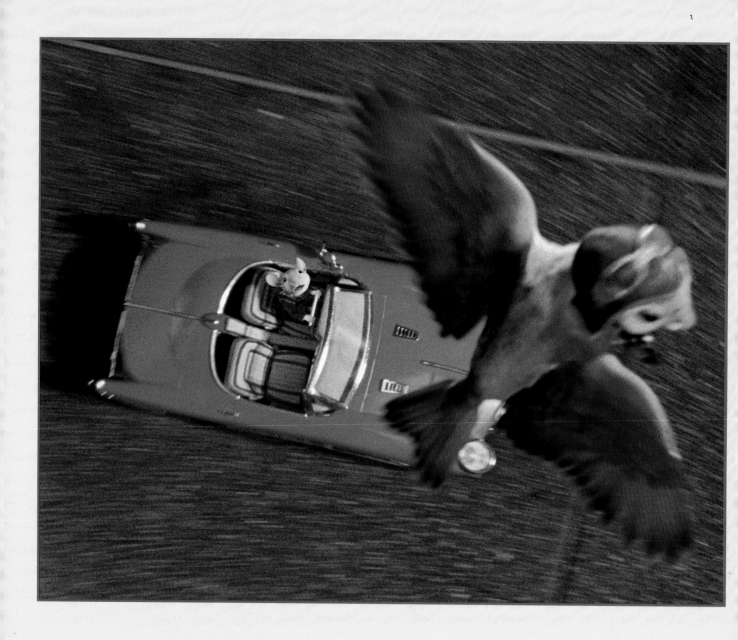

Happily, Stuart's car was still working.
Beep-beep!

While he was driving home from
school one day . . . *Crash!* A little bird
fell from the sky into his car.

She was being chased by an angry falcon. Stuart and his speedy red roadster rescued the unexpected passenger.

The bird yelled at the falcon as they drove off, "Eat my feathers, you vile buzzard!"

Zoom-zoom!

Stuart's expert driving helped them escape the falcon.

"We did it!" cried the grateful bird. "Or should I say, *you* did it?"

"Yeah!" said Stuart proudly. "I did."

Stuart introduced himself and brought the bird home. Her name was Margalo. Stuart tended her hurt wing. He had made a new friend.

At the Little house, Margalo
settled into a comfy jewelry box.

"I'll just stay till my wing heals,"
said Margalo.

"Stay as long as you like," offered
Mrs. Little.

All the Littles were very welcoming, except for Snowbell.

Guests are like fish, he thought. *After two days, they start to stink!*

Chapter 2

Missing Margalo

Margalo fit right in with the Little family. She liked to play games and sing songs as much as they did.

Stuart was happy to have a friend of his own—especially one who was his own size.

"You're as big as you feel," Margalo
told him.

Stuart began to believe her.

One day, Mrs. Little was washing the dishes when she noticed she was missing her diamond ring.

"It could have gone down the drain!" she cried.

Stuart wanted to go look for the ring, but Mr. Little was worried.

"I don't know Stuart. It's awfully dark down there," he said.

"Come on, Dad, let me try," said Stuart.

Mr. Little fashioned a hook and string to lower brave Stuart into the drain.

"How is it down there so far?" asked George.

"Wet," replied Stuart.

Suddenly, the string holding the hook broke. *Ker-plunk!* Stuart was trapped at the bottom of the drain.

The Little family searched the kitchen but could not find any more string to rescue Stuart. Then Margalo opened the clasp on Mrs. Little's necklace and lowered it down the drain. Stuart grabbed the necklace, and Margalo lifted him to safety.

Hooray! All the Littles were happy to have Stuart back.

"Margalo, you're the best friend I ever had," said Stuart.

Margalo felt bad. She knew where the ring really was, but she couldn't tell Stuart.

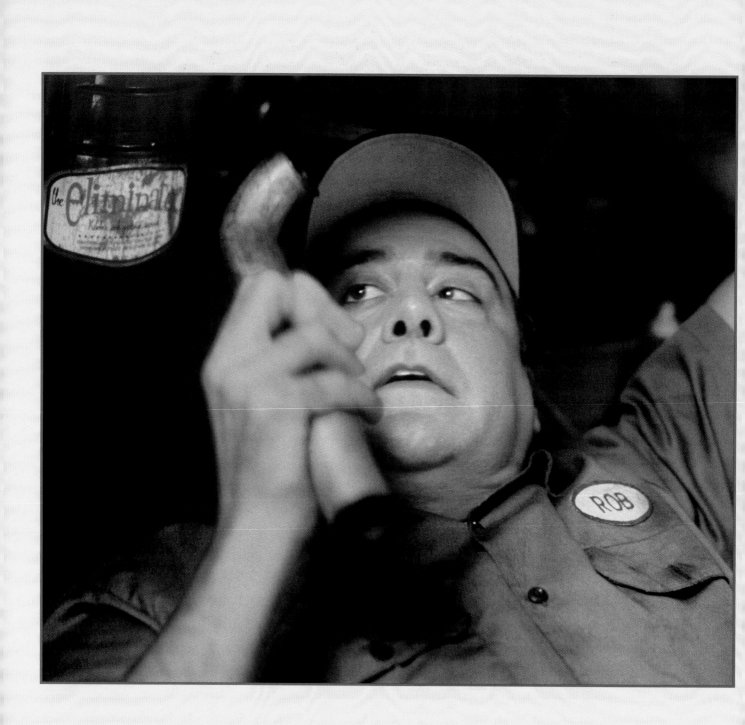

The next day, the Littles called a plumber to check the drain. But the ring was not there.

And now Margalo was missing, too!

"I can't find her anywhere," said Stuart.

"Maybe she just felt it was time to go,"
Mr. Little said gently.

Stuart did not believe that could be true.

That night, Stuart could not sleep.

"I think I know what happened to Margalo," Stuart told George. "The falcon got her!"

Stuart knew he had to save Margalo.

"Stuart . . ." George said awkwardly. "She's just a bird."

"No, George," said Stuart. "She's my friend. And when you're friends with Stuart Little, you're friends for life."

Stuart convinced Snowbell to join his adventure in the big city.

Down a dirty, dark alley, Stuart and Snowbell found Monty.

Monty was just the type of rough-and-tumble streetcat that would know where the falcon lived.

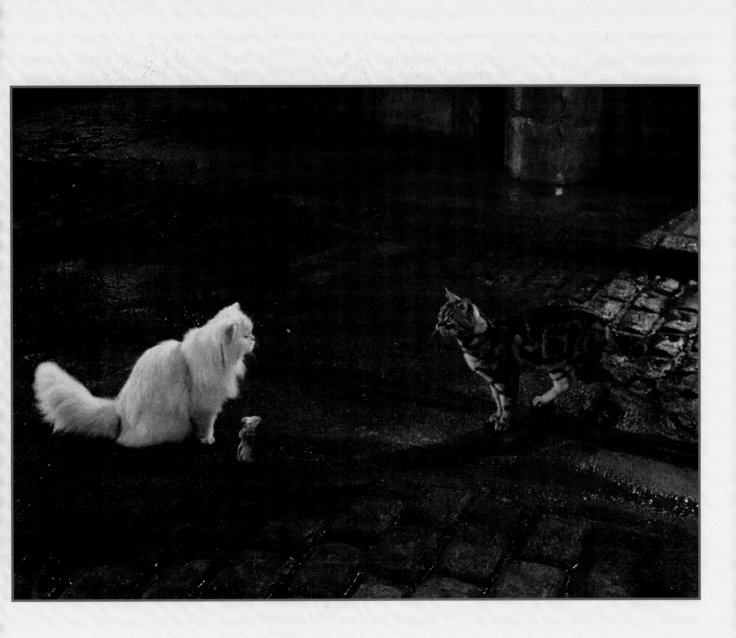

"Falcon? The jewel thief?" cried Monty. "You don't want to find him!"

Stuart persisted, and finally, Monty told them that Falcon lived across the park at the top of the Pishkin Building.

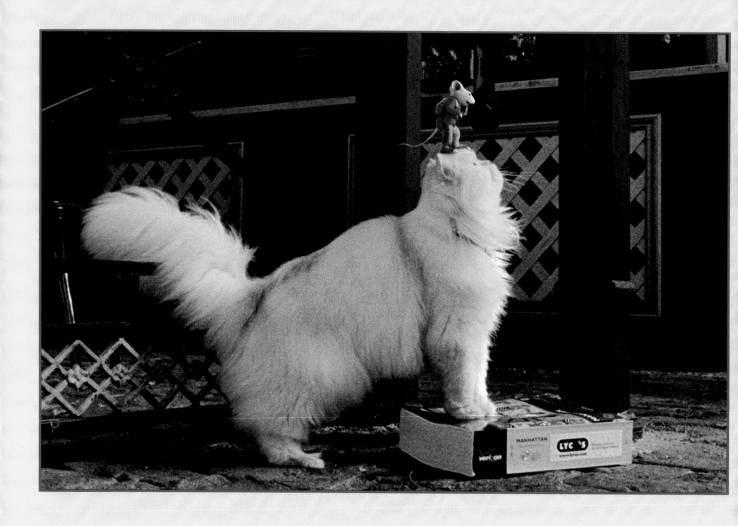

Stuart quickly phoned George to let his brother know where he was going. Then Stuart and Snowbell made their way to the Pishkin building. But how could they get up to the top?

"I'll think of something," Stuart told Snowbell. And that's just what he did.

Stuart attached a small paper cup to a balloon. Then he boarded the cup. Up, up, up, he floated.

"You can do it!" called Snowbell. To himself, he added, "This has 'fiasco' written all over it."

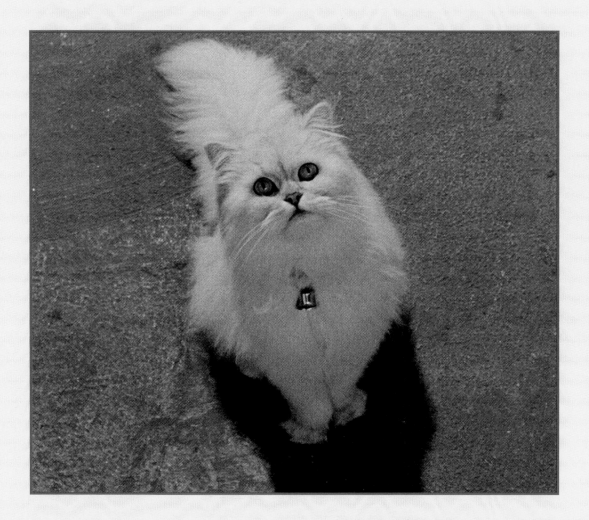

Stuart carefully stepped out of the
paper cup and onto the roof.

"Margalo, are you up here?" he called.

Suddenly, Falcon appeared. Margalo
was with him.

"She does what I tell her," Falcon growled. Stuart could not believe that Margalo worked for Falcon!

Falcon did not give Margalo time to explain. He grabbed Stuart in his talons.

"Don't hurt him, Falcon!" pleaded Margalo.

Falcon ignored her. He carried Stuart to the edge of the building . . . and let go.

"No!" cried Margalo.

Far below, Stuart landed in the back of a garbage truck.

Chapter 3

Stuart to the Rescue

Stuart wound up on a stinky, slimy trash barge.

"I know a Little is always supposed to see a silver lining," Stuart told himself, but this time it was hard for him to believe. "Maybe this means I'm not really a Little. Maybe I'm Stuart . . . Nobody."

Stuart felt about as low and little as he ever had before.

Then suddenly . . . the silver lining! Buried in the trash was Stuart's airplane—the one George had thrown away!

Could Stuart make it fly again?

While Stuart was stuck on the trash barge, George finally told his parents that Stuart had gone to the Pishkin Building to save Margalo.

The Littles jumped into a taxi to search for Stuart.

Everyone was worried about the middle Little. Mr. Little tried to stay hopeful. "We don't have to assume the worst," he said. "After all, it's not the Little way."

Far above the worried family, Margalo told Falcon, "I'm through doing what you tell me to do. I'm leaving you, Falcon. Forever!"

Margalo grabbed Mrs. Little's ring—she had stolen it for Falcon. Now she was going to take it back where it belonged.

Angrily, Falcon flew after Margalo. He was about to grab her when he heard . . . *Putt-putt-putt!* Stuart scooped Margalo into his plane!

"Stuart you're alive!" Margalo cried happily.

"So far," said Stuart.

Falcon screeched after them at top speed. Stuart flew wildly, diving and weaving. It was no use. Falcon was gaining on them.

Then Stuart had an idea. First he got Margalo safely out of the plane. Next Stuart headed his plane straight toward Falcon! Bird and plane flew faster and faster toward a collision.

Just before impact, Stuart used the diamond in his mother's ring to reflect sunlight into Falcon's eyes. A dazed Falcon crashed into the plane, just after Stuart had leaped out.

"Bye-bye, birdbrain!" called Stuart, using his tablecloth as a parachute. Falcon fell to the ground. He never bothered anyone again.

"Stuart!" cheered the happy Little family, who had arrived at the park just in time to witness his heroics.

Margalo returned Mrs. Little's ring.

"I took it," she confessed.

"And now she's giving it back," Stuart said kindly.

"I'm just glad to have all of you back," added Mrs. Little. When Snowbell found the happy group, the family was complete.

Stuart and Margalo were good friends. They knew each other well. When the summer ended, Stuart noticed how much Margalo wanted to head south with the other birds. He urged her to follow her dream.

"I'll miss you, Stuart," she said before flying off.

Watching her go, Mr. Little wondered out loud, "What's the silver lining this time?"

"She'll be back in the spring," Stuart answered.

Stuart smiled. However far Margalo
flew, Stuart would always carry her
friendship in his great big, Little heart.